JOY in SMALL THINGS

-Moments of Everyday Happiness

Nyra Publishers

Joy In Small Things: Moments of Everyday Happiness

All Global Publishing rights are held by

NYRA PUBLISHERS LLP

www.nyrapublishers.com

Published in July 2025 India.

Dorathy Ch Marak, Debjani Roychowdhury, Shreya Ghosh, Gilliane Marie Damasco, Kadambari Gupta, Vijay Gupta

Cover Design and Image: Editing Team, Nyra Publishers

Interior Layout and Design: Editing Team, Nyra Publishers

ISBN: 9788198967824

First Edition

Foreword

In a world that often moves too fast, we tend to forget that happiness is not always loud or extravagant. It doesn't always arrive with fanfare or celebration. More often, it tiptoes in quietly—hiding in a moment of silence, a warm glance, a shared cup of tea, or the sunlight resting on your windowsill.

Joy in Small Things – Moments of Everyday Happiness is a gentle reminder to notice. To pause. To feel. This anthology brings together voices from all walks of life who have turned their gaze inward, and outward, to capture the beauty that hides in plain sight. Each page invites the reader to rediscover joy in its most subtle and sincere forms—be it through poetry, prose, or a fleeting reflection.

At Nyra Publishers, we believe in the power of stories not just to entertain, but to heal, to soothe, and to reconnect us with what truly matters. This collection does just that. It doesn't aim to impress with grandeur, but rather to touch hearts with truth.

As you read, may you be reminded of your own small joys—the ones that arrive without asking and stay with you forever. Happy Reading...

Nyra Publishers
June 2025

Table of Contents

Dorathy Ch Marak

"A Call Deferred"

Found her sweet and charismatic.
Her laugh, a giggle pure with hilarity. Petite, slim,
a sun-kissed porcelain glow; a charm you want to
keep.
Been good to me or maybe I'm just her kind.

A phone call away? NOT really.
It takes time_ an hour, maybe two_ sometimes it
dribbles into three ,or quadruples.

Calls return
But never in haste.
The message , though always finds it's way.

In quiet moments,
I wish I hadn't called .
The waiting gnaws at me, vexing the heart, while
patience falters fooling me happily.

But this _
This is LIFE.
Life whispers lessons;
To master patience_ their meaning unfolding with
age.
Be it that you seek to learn or not, life weaves
lessons in silence..

SMILING through the STORM

Palettes kiss her pale cheeks and tinted lips tear the
moroseness away.
She steps into morning, clothed in colours;
Never brooding, never succumbing to the shadows
where sorrow softly speaks.

Once a bond, bright and blessed;
now sitting in dim light.
A beauty queen draped in a weary gown,
a fawn lost in the glade.
Grace still a stranger ;
entangled in the delicate shreds of a fractured mind.

"Joie de vivre", she sighs in echoes so small.
While within her paracosm, she builds up the wall.
The callow dancer swings her arms with dismay-
"Alackaday!" she cries, as the colours slip away.

She glows in the sun, a radiant muse; embracing
daylight in vibrant hues.
As the night exhales its hush
the shadows slip inside her skin.
Her wide, wandering mind wrestles with the thinning
light of faith.

She hears them coming again- those echoes, robust;
whispers of doubt amid the fading trust.
Where dreams once thrives, now fear takes the throne,
Eroded strings strumming memories whole.

She secures herself in her heterotopia-
A realm full of life, colours, a vibrant utopia. In this

world she loves, each moment's a treasure:
Customised stones- each a story to tell.

In this crafted world where sorrows take flight;
a true eccedentesiast rises -
smiling against every odds.

Debjani Roychowdhury

The Moment

(Roseline you are definitely going to falter and regret in your later phases for this one decision, just mark my words") After few minutes of facing this inner turmoil of her thoughts from her brief conversation with her long - term friend cum boyfriend Hemant 3 hours ago at inside a Cafe cum small Restaurant; Roseline stood up from the Garden bench where she sat for half an hour to introspect again on the important step that she is going to take tomorrow morning and then said aloud to herself "Here what matters is my state of mind after deciding to adopt Suman from that Orphanage where I work as a Receptionist. I am quite optimistic regarding my this bold decision and I would be till the end and the matter ends here".

Next day morning, a 12 years old boy is tying his long wavy hairs with a rubber band wearing a ladies jeans pant with a cream- coloured t-shirt written 'Girls Are Pink'. A lady caretaker came inside the room where the children dwells and asked , "Suman , you must have got yourself dressed up by now?" Suman shockingly looked at her with a baffled expression as if he is confused about what to reply. Then at the meantime, Roseline enters the room behind that lady and said confidently, "I think he is definitely ready, come Suman let's go to home". He confusedly looked at her with his not too small but slightly little in size than being bigger eyes and asked slowly in a reaction mixed with society infused shamefulness and fear, "Can you buy me a teddy on the way to your home?" Roseline replied with a light smile on her face, "No, don't say it like this, say it as "Our House" yes my son, my dear little son with a golden heart just as a girl like me. From now on, we will stay together permanently with lots of chats and conversations and lots and lots of shopping's and marketings that we will do together everyday, yes, will not slip it in any single days okay. So, let's not delay our journey further come let's go she said so by offering her right hand to him so that he could hold her hand without any hesitation. Suman slowly stepped out his hand to give into hers and then again Roseline said in assurance, "Yes I will buy you your teddy and also a bouquet full of roses to welcome your arrival in the house. Because you have given me the best gift of my life by accepting me as your Guardian Mother, I am feeling like I am only your real Mother who was waiting to embrace you since a long ago and finally now it happened. You are now my Son, Suman Mehra.

After a taxi journey of 5 to 10 miles they entered into the house. Upon his first arrival, Suman was welcomed by a 20 years old tomboyish girl wearing black hoody jacket inside of it a blue track suit and pant, "Oh so this is my Nephew Suman?" Roseline, "Yes Melina, this is my Son Suman. Suman meet your Aunt Melina, you two would surely create a great bond together, isn't it Sister?" Melina, "Yes offcourse Rosie! There is no doubt in it, come Suman let me give you a detailed tour of our house, come!". All of them went inside and after some minutes of interacting together both Melina and Suman became quickly close and Frank with each other and even they were smiling and laughing a lot on little fun gossips and conversations with great joy and happiness. Watching the duo enjoying each other's company and seeing their matched heartful vibes she got melted into tears and then realised that enjoying the smallest and little things in life is more important than listening to any people's advice based on their fleeting and bad gazes. She again thought that luckily she got back that lively enthusiasm and smile again on her Sister's face which got lost due to her inferiority complex of being boyish in nature which is contrary to her female gender and at the same time also satisfied her cravings to be a mother for a long time which her boyfriend Hemant can't fulfil to her as he refused to marry her because he don't want any kind of full - time commitments in his relationships. She silently accepted that and decided to go for adoption and become a single mother to her lovely child and she already has started that journey of becoming a responsible single mother in her life. “I did it, I did it already and will continue to do it with grace and glory and built my child stronger than any other normal person, goodbye Hemant now I don't need any annoying person in my life. What I need is only and only my family that is my Sister and my lovely Son Suman” She cheerfully joined both her Sister and Son in their playful fun banters and chit - chats.

Shreya Ghosh

Joyful Journey

Fun filled with joy;
Merrier happiness;
Smile with lots of emotions;
Crops with greenery grasslands;
Glow of thoughts with sparks of emotions;
Grasses decorated with moving image;
Glasses decorated with beauty;
Children immensely playing with paper boats
Melodious voice of echoes from flute buzzing;
Heavy storm of snowfall filled like chains;
Enjoying together in the yellow sand dunes;
With soften music voice flattened with colours of glory;
Sea beach empower with water flowing;
Glaze of happiness of thoughts from imagination;
Sunlight empower with light of glory;
Golden thoughts changes with sparks of happiness;
Peace and calm of emotions with glow of thoughts;
With the soften music voice flattened in mind;

Green crops field with shadow of water;

Glazed of animals from valleys;

Women collecting from bushes of the valley;

Children immensely enjoying together with playful banter

Whispering of plants blowing happily;

Farmers ploughing and ploughing with a smile;

Echoes of voice erupt from the empty fields;

Children enjoying the rainfall;

Flower garden with a fragrance of sweet smell;

Surrounded by amazed chains of joyful moments with a thoughts of happiness;

Sweet dreams unfolds in the yellow green mellow meadows enjoying with sand dunes of imagination;

Stars whispering in the sky with a beaming of light.

Gilliane Marie Damasco

The Smallest Things

When I was younger,
I would go out to look for my father,
Who sat outside our house at night.
He would tell me tales about the stars,
And fascinating stories of the planet Mars—
My little self would listen with delight.

When the lights went out without a hint,
The candle's glow became our glint,
While Mother sang to soothe the quiet night.
We'd make hand-shadow puppets play,
Hear crickets chirp the dark away—
And ghost stories gave us such a fright.

Being young can truly
Make us live so freely,
Unaware of what the future brings.
But now that I have stepped into
The dreams my younger self once knew,
I find that I miss the smallest things.

We are often told to dream big and aim for the sky,
That life will be so much better when you are up high.

Sure, there is some truth in that, won't you agree?
But joy is not just found in flight,
Nor only in the grandest height—
Being up there is not the only way to be happy.

So when life gets tough,
And going on just feels too rough,
Breathe, pause a while, and take a break.
Notice the little things you often miss,
Let tiny moments bring you bliss.
Life will always be beautiful as long as we're awake.

Kadambari Gupta

JOY IN SMALL THINGS

When the night is woken up by the rising sun a
bright light from the balcony arrives ,

A new day that breathes new life in the lake of
positivity this heart takes a dive,

Having breakfast that feeds the soul made with
ingredients of affection love and care,

Holding that cup of coffee with cream in these
hands what more could this heart even ask for.

Getting drenched in the rain playing with those
rain drops brings smile on this face in a fraction of
few seconds,

Writing down thoughts in a journal with a pen and
ink, a dialogue is exchanged with those blank
pages each word written on paper.

In the handwriting as neat as a project that will get
great grades from the teacher. the conversation
with those pages make us calm

Every achievement , each point of progress
achieved glows like diamonds , when with the
journal is shared, who keeps all our secrets safe
and sound.

Walking in the garden ,today saw an old couple
taking a walk, they held each other's trembling
hands , this gesture shows assurance, don't worry
won't let you

Fall whether there are stones in the way or a heap of sand, in the same garden these eyes see a, mother with a baby in her arms, the laughs of the angel

Is enough to bring relief and peace to this tired soul.

Singing your favourite melody ,and dancing your heart out latching the door of the room

Looking at those pictures years old and reminiscing the incident that happened when these pictures were clicked,

In all these ,moments joy is experienced as they just required a heart to experience ,today as humans are lost in their screens and gadgets

Looking forward to check the number of followers on their social media pages , the count begins from number of likes , and comments

Then filters are applied to match up to those standards set up by the social media,

, a load of expensive make-up ,outfits and accessories from online stores is supplied , in this artificial world we are living in today

Our joy is also artificial and when the photos don't receive required number of likes , a whole line of negative comments are seen , this world breaks and depression is felt

So take a pause from the scrolling , your phone ,
find joy in everyday life as you once did when
there were no smart phones and internet, go out of
the house see there

Are things , experiences that will provide. warm
fizzles,

real, joy is not in swanky, cars, diamonds and
branded bags, joy lies in our everyday life you
knew this concept when started writing about it in
the beginning yet when the lens of comparison
and greed

Is worn joy is an exam to experience each day
today just change your lens and wear the old ones
again, meet your friends laugh sing dance with
them as loud as the beats of this heart can hear, all
negativity will be released in the sky

Darkness from life will bid goodbye as you saw joy
in things small which are too precious and
expensive to be purchased from the mall.

Vijay Gupta

बड़ी देर लगायी आते आते!

Adapted from 'What took you so long' by John Roedel!

कल रात मैंने 'ख़ुद' से पूछा
क्या तुम दिल और दिमाग़ की आपसी जंग से परेशान हो?
क्या इनमें से किसी के साथ और रह पाने की सोच से भी हैरान हो?

मैंने बिन बोले अपनी मायूसी कुछ यूँ बताई।
मेरा दिल जो 'कल' गुज़र गया उसको सोच उदास चलता है,
और दिमाग़ आने वाले 'कल' की ज़दोज़हेद से डरता है।
और मेरा वजूद कभी दिल और कभी दिमाग़ के साथ असमंजस में रहता है।।

तब मेरा वो 'ख़ुद' मेरी हथेली दबा बोला,
अपने फेफड़ों के साथ कुछ समय गुज़ार!

यदि तुम्हारा दिल जाने वाले और दिमाग़ आने वाले 'कल' से रखता तुम्हें परेशान है।
तो फेफड़ों के पास तुम्हारी समस्या का समाधान है।।

फेफड़ों में ना वो ‘कल’ रहता हैं ना ये ‘कल’ होता है।
वहाँ केवल आज होता है।
लंबी सांस अंदर, लंबी साँस बाहर।
आज, यहाँ, ये, वर्तमान केवल,
ये क्षण, ये पल।।

और इस पल इस क्षण में सुस्ता लो,
ज़िंदगी थोड़ी टिक जाने दो।
दिल और दिमाग़ को अपनी जंग निबटाने दो।।

मैंने अपना छोटा सा बस्ता लगाया।
और दिल जहां पुरानी तस्वीरों में उलझा था,
दिमाग़ नयी तस्वीरों के रंगो से डरता था,
मैंने फेफड़ों का दरवाज़ा खटखटाया।।

प्यारी सी मुस्कान से उसने तुरंत बुलाया।
एक लंबी, खुली साँस ले गले से लगाया।।
फिर बस एक ही बात बोली,
बड़ी देर लगायी, आते आते!

About the Authors

Dorathy Ch Marak

Dorathy Ch Marak. Born and brought up in Meghalaya, Garo Hills Region of Tura, has Studied Master of Arts in English Literature in NEHU Tura and won the Rector Gold Medallist too. She is a State B.Ed. topper (Tenth Rank) and currently a (PhD) scholar in NEHU Tura (English Department)

About the Author
Debjani Roychowdhury

Debjani Roychowdhury is a Writer who writes Short Stories, Poems and also Long Part Series in Pratilipi English App on any kind of genres needed or wanted to be read. She has ranked in 9th position on the Short Story Competition on Teachers' Day in 2023 arranged by Pratilipi English Team Online and has also got a digital certificate shortly after that. My earlier published works with Nyra Publishers are "Affectionate Echoes: A Romantic Anthology Volume 1", "Haunted Whispers: A Horror Anthology", "Shades Of Summer" and 2 others.

About the Author
Shreya Ghosh

Shreya Ghosh. Born in 23rd October in 1993. Completed graduation from WBSU in 2018. Writing is journey of words and creations. My first writing journey started with people's reflections live online writing competition. Second with The wordings, Blue star publication, Nyra publication, Gyan publication blue cloud publication and many other publications

About the Author
Gilliane Marie Damasco

Gilliane is an aspiring Filipino writer with a deep passion for creative writing. She enjoys crafting poems and short stories, and dreams of publishing a novel one day. Having written on Wattpad under the username @GaileLin, she took a break due to academic commitments but now aims to return to her writing journey and fulfil her lifelong dream of becoming a published writer and inspire souls through her works.

About the Author

Kadambari Gupta

She is, P.G, LL.B. by qualification and a writer by passion is a published co -author of over eleven hundred and sixty anthologies, and wishes to continue this pious bond with her pen and paper.

About the Author

Vijay Gupta

An HR leader by profession, but at heart — a poet, storyteller, and theatre enthusiast. Husband to a wonderfully accomplished wife, and a proud father to two incredible daughters and their equally amazing partners. Despite the years, still nervous, still unsure — especially in the company of younger, bolder poets and performers who leave me inspired (and often in awe). Recently stepped onto the stage with my recitations — a late beginning, but a heartfelt one. Hopeful of seeing my words in print soon. A food lover through and through... and yes, it does show!